The Most World Records

by Annie Auerbach
illustrated by Gary Johnson

TITLE I DEPARTMENT PROGRAM
FUNDED P.L. 107-110
GOVERNMENT P.L.

Simon Spotlight / Nickelodeon

New York   London   Toronto   Sydney   Singapore

Based on the TV series *CatDog*®
created by Peter Hannan as seen on Nickelodeon®

SIMON SPOTLIGHT
An imprint of Simon & Schuster Children's Publishing Division
1230 Avenue of the Americas, New York, New York 10020

Manufactured in the United States of America

First Edition

2 4 6 8 10 9 7 5 3 1

ISBN 0-689-83465-9

Library of Congress Catalog Card Number 00-133440

Chapter One

History was about to be made in Nearburg. It all started at CatDog's house. . . .

Early one morning, Cat was reading the newspaper. Dog, on the other hand, was reading the back of the cereal box.

Suddenly Cat slammed the newspaper down on the kitchen table. Kavity Krunch cereal went everywhere. "This is it!" he exclaimed.

Dog ran around and tried to catch the cereal in his mouth as it came falling down.

"Dog, did you hear me?" Cat asked excitedly.

"What?" Dog replied, with a mouthful of cereal.

"We are finally going to make a name for ourselves—a *good* name, that is," Cat explained.

"Huh?" asked a confused Dog.

"Listen to this," Cat said. "Nearburg is pleased to announce the first annual Most World Records Contest. The team that wins the most world records will be awarded $50,000, a million-dollar home, a lifetime supply of Kavity Krunch cereal, and will go down in history!"

Cat turned to Dog. "Isn't that incredible?!"

"Wow, wow, wow!" shouted Dog. "A lifetime supply of Kavity Krunch!"

"Forget the cereal," said Cat. "Just think of all that money—and we'd be famous around the world!"

"Not to mention Nearburg!" Dog added.

"We'd be rich, we'd be famous, we'd be the toast of the town," Cat said dreamily.

"Toast?" said Dog, licking his lips.

"Calm down, Dog. It's just an expression."

"Oh," said Dog, a little disappointed.

"Come on, let's go to city hall and sign up for the competition." Then Cat looked at Dog's sad face and added, "Afterward, we can go to Burrito Bucket and celebrate our upcoming win!"

"Taco, taco, taco . . . ," Dog began to chant as they headed out the door.

Cat was humming his own tune. "Fame and fortune, fame and fortune . . ."

Chapter Two

City hall was buzzing with activity. Everyone in Nearburg was talking about the upcoming Most World Records Contest. Large signs explained that the two-day series of contests was divided into five categories: smarts, games, bizarre-and-unusual, dance, and food.

Cat snickered. "With my brains and your appetite, Dog," he began, "we'll be able to ace the smarts and food contests."

"But what about the other categories?" Dog wondered aloud.

Cat continued, "Well, I always win when we play games, and we're both very good dancers—"

"And we're already bizarre and unusual!" Dog chimed in.

"That's the spirit!" Cat told his brother.

As CatDog got in line, Cat looked around. Then he whispered to Dog, "These poor contestants. They don't know what they're up against."

"What are they up against?" asked Dog.

"ME!" exclaimed Cat. "Uh . . . I mean, us."

Unfortunately, their conversation was overheard—by the Greasers!

"Yous two here to get a poundin' in front of everybody?" asked Cliff.

"Heh, heh . . . I love a show," said Lube. "Especially if it's a poundin'!"

"Hiya, Dog," Shriek said. "What are you still doing hanging around that lousy cat? Why don't you join our team?"

"Then at least you'd have a *chance* of winnin'," added Cliff.

Cat pushed Dog aside. "Dog is with me," Cat told the Greasers.

Dog was touched that his brother was defending him. "Yeah," he said. "We make a great team. Cat loves having me on his team."

"Well, I wouldn't go that far," Cat said. "But, Dog's on *my* team. So prepare to lose, Greasers!"

"We'll see who gets da prizes and who's crying dere eyes out," said Cliff.

"Yeah . . . crybaby," added Lube.

"Next!" said a voice behind them.

It was CatDog's turn to register!

They were handed a seventeen-page application and a huge 649-page book of the rules. Cat could barely lift it.

"There's no shorter version?" asked Cat.

"How about a videotape instead?"

suggested Dog. "I love movies. Maybe one starring Mean Bob?"

But the official just shook his head.

"Oh, well," said Cat. "Come on, Dog. Since you're on my team, *you* get to carry the rule book home."

"Are we still going to Burrito Bucket?" asked Dog as he lugged the gigantic book.

"Sure," Cat answered. "You're going to need all the energy you can get."

Chapter Three

With a stomach full of tacos, CatDog finally made it home. Dog had to push the enormous rulebook up the hill to their house. As soon as they got inside, Dog fell asleep. He was exhausted!

Meanwhile, Cat filled out the long application and then read *all* 649 pages of the rulebook. Most of it seemed to be nonsense, so Cat picked out the rules he liked.

"Dog, wake up," called Cat. "I need to explain the rules to you."

Dog stretched. "But I thought you said we were going to win with no problem," he said.

"Of course we will!" Cat declared. "But we still need to know the rules."

"Okeydokey," said Dog. "But give me the short version—the really short version."

"Rule number one: Teams must have at least two members," Cat explained.

"That's easy for us," said Dog. "We love doing everything together, right? Cat? Cat?"

Cat rolled his eyes. "Yeah, yeah . . . everything . . . together."

Suddenly Dog looked worried and asked, "What if we're up against a bigger team?"

"Relax," said Cat. "Rule number two states that not all the members compete in each event. And how many times do I have to tell you—we will win! No problem! Remember that you've got *me* on your team!"

"Oh, yeah!" said Dog.

"Rule number three says that cheating is not allowed," Cat continued.

"I hope the Greasers read that rule over and over!" said Dog.

"Ha!" Cat laughed. "You know reading is not one of their strong points!" Then he said, "Okay, here's the last important rule: Mayor Rancid Rabbit will be the one and only judge. All rules can change if Rancid feels like it. Isn't that ridiculous?"

"Well, he *is* the mayor," Dog pointed out.

"If he can change all the rules, why did I bother reading the huge rule book?!" exclaimed Cat.

Suddenly Winslow came out of his hole in the wall. "Hiya, CatDog. What's goin' on?"

"Me and Cat are going to get a lifetime supply of Kavity Krunch cereal!" exclaimed Dog.

"Oh, you entered that big contest?" asked Winslow.

Cat narrowed his eyes. "So, you know about it?"

"Of course," Winslow replied with a smirk. "I've been approached to join many of the teams. It helps to be small, you know."

Instantly, Cat wondered if Winslow would be helpful to his team—even though he hated the little blue rat.

Cat had to think fast. He knew that winning was the most important thing, at any cost. "Well, what if I offered you five percent of the winnings?" he said to Winslow.

"Ten percent," Winslow countered. He was always looking to make a quick buck.

"Seven," said Cat.

"Nine," said Winslow.

"Seven and three quarters," offered Cat.

"Eight and a half," said Winslow, "and that's my final offer."

Cat gritted his teeth. "Er . . . deal," he finally said, shaking Winslow's hand.

"Now it's time to get to work," said Cat. "We have a lot of preparing to do!"

"*You* have a lot of preparing to do," corrected Winslow. "*I* have a hot date with a very special rodent. See ya." And off he went.

Cat was annoyed. "That ratboy better come through when we need him!" He sighed. "I guess we're going to have to be the brains behind this operation." Then he looked at Dog who was asleep again. "Well, *I'll* have to be the brains."

Chapter Four

The next few weeks were filled with nonstop preparations. CatDog followed a strict schedule to make sure they were in tip-top shape for all the contests.

To prepare for the smarts competitions, Cat read book after book, filled notebooks with math equations, studied hundreds of flash cards, and even listened to audio tapes while he slept.

Dog did his part, too. He worked on his fetching abilities, blowing his biggest bubble gum bubble, and of course, he practiced his favorite hobby: eating.

For Dog, this training was a blast. For Cat, it was serious business. He wasn't about

to lose to anyone—especially not the Greasers! In fact, the contest was so important to Cat that he didn't mind when Dog ran after a ball or chased a garbage truck. "It's all part of the training," he told himself. "And it'll all be worth it when we win!"

When the big day arrived, Cat was more confident than ever.

"Kiss this old life good-bye, Dog," Cat said. "By the end of tomorrow, everyone will be jealous of our new million-dollar house, our money, our—"

"Cat? Cat!" said Dog. "We have to *win* the contest first."

"Details, details," Cat laughed. "It'll be a piece of cake."

"Yum," Dog said dreamily. "I love cake!"

"Later, Dog. We'd better get going," said Cat. "Hey, where's Winslow?"

CatDog knocked on his door and

looked around the house. But there was no sign of Winslow anywhere.

"Maybe he's already at city hall," Dog suggested. "Let's go!"

Everyone in Nearburg came out to cheer the winners and laugh at the losers. TV cameras and news reporters were everywhere. There were five teams that were going to compete. Originally there were more teams, but many of them quit when they saw the rulebook—and the Greasers!

As the five teams began to arrive, the crowd went wild. All of the TV crews scrambled to get interviews with each team.

"Hello, this is Barbara Dingleberry from Channel NRBG," said one reporter. "I'm here with one of the teams. Could you tell us your names? Hello? Sir? Ma'am? Hello?"

But the four-member team seemed to freeze as soon as they saw the TV cameras. They were more than just tongue-tied—they were petrified!

Eventually, four stretchers were brought in and the team was taken away.

"Good," said Cliff. "One team down, and we haven't even started yet."

"Dis is gonna be easy!" added Shriek.

Just then, Barbara Dingleberry poked her head—and her microphone—right between the Greasers. "I'm here with the Greaser dog team: Cliff, Lube, and Shiek."

"Dat's Shriek, lady," growled Shriek.

"Hey . . . Shriek's no lady," shouted Cat.

"How 'bout a knuckle sandwich?" Shriek threatened Cat.

Everyone turned to look at Cat. Suddenly there was a microphone and a TV

camera in Cat's face. Luckily, he loved the spotlight.

"And what team are you part of?" the reporter asked.

"The winning team—the CatDog team," answered Cat.

"And which competition are you most confident about?" asked the reporter.

"All of them," Cat replied. "The other teams don't stand a chance."

"Yous not gonna be able to stand when dis competition is done!" yelled Cliff.

"It seems like you have some pretty stiff competition," the reporter said to Cat.

"Yeah, stiff in the brain, perhaps," Cat laughed.

The Greasers lunged for Cat but Dog quickly took off.

"Gotta go!" yelled Cat. "We'll sign autographs after we win!"

Chapter Five

"May I have your attention, please?" said Mr. Sunshine, the mayor's right-hand man.

But no one heard him. They were all too excited, chattering to each other.

"Quiet down," Mr. Sunshine said.

Still, no one heard him.

"I said quiet down," Mr. Sunshine repeated.

The noise *still* didn't die down.

"SHUT UP!" Mayor Rancid finally yelled.

The entire population of Nearburg turned to him in shock. There was dead silence.

"That's better," Mayor Rancid said. Then

to Mr. Sunshine he whispered, "You gotta work on your people skills, kid."

Rancid cleared his throat and said, "Now, I'd like to welcome all of you to Nearburg's first annual Most World Records Contest. The team with the most world records will not only take home some million-dollar prizes, but will also go down in history."

Cat wasn't listening to the mayor's speech. He was looking around at the other teams, sizing up the competition. There were three other teams: the Greasers, Eddie the Squirrel and some of his pals, and Mervis and Dunglap. "Well, Mervis and Dunglap are useless. I don't have to worry about them," Cat thought to himself. "But where is that Winslow? I'm not giving him eight-and-half percent for nothing."

". . . and so, in my opinion, being a

good sport is overrated," Mayor Rancid continued. "It's all about winning— winning with a capital *W*."

"Yeah!" the crowd cheered.

"Losers are just that, losers!" Rancid declared. "Whoever said, 'It's not about winning or losing, it's how you play the game' must have been a loser!"

"Yeah! Loser!" the crowd cheered.

"Like CatDog!" added Cliff.

"Yeah!" the crowd cheered.

"Ha!" Cat shouted. "You'll all see! Victory will be mine! Uh . . . I mean ours!"

"Yeah!" Dog yelled in support.

"And now, I'd like to introduce our very special host for this two-day event," said Rancid. "All the way from *Sports Off-Center*, Mr. Randolph Grant!"

Everyone went wild! They were all fans of his daily sports show.

"Well, hello there, sports fans," began Randolph. "It's a pleasure to be here. Really, it is. And may I say that I think this series of contests will be a great achievement in Nearburg history. I just *love* it!"

Mayor Rancid took the microphone back. "Will the four remaining teams please come forward," he instructed.

The Greasers, CatDog, Eddie's team, and Mervis and Dunglap all came forward.

"Good luck," Dog said to Mervis.

"Gee, thanks," Mervis replied. "And good luck to you, too."

"We don't need luck," said Cat. Then he elbowed Dog. "Hey, don't talk to the enemy."

"That's not the enemy," Dog replied. "That's Mervis."

Cat sighed. "Just focus on winning, okay?"

"Whatever you say, Cat," said Dog.

Rancid was glaring at CatDog. "If you

two don't mind, I'd like to finish my speech!" Rancid said sternly. "Now, Randolph will be giving us the play-by-play, but remember that *I* have final word on the rules. Now, go out there and break some records!"

Chapter Six

With a bang, the competitions began!

Randolph grabbed the microphone. "And here we are, smarts fans, we're making history," he said in his best sportscaster voice. "First up is the smarts category. The team with the most correct answers in each category wins that category. Just buzz in when you know the answer."

"No problem," Cat said confidently.

Mr. Sunshine read the questions to the teams.

There were many kinds of questions on a variety of subjects. Shriek got points for guessing right at the true-false questions. Dog almost scored with the environmental questions. He had an impressive knowledge of different types of garbage. But so did the Greaser dogs, who won that round.

Eddie's team kept trying to answer questions, but Cliff kept giving Eddie the evil eye. Eddie idolized Cliff and would do anything to become a Greaser dog—even though he was a squirrel. Eventually, Eddie and his team stopped trying to answer questions at all.

Mervis and Dunglap only answered one question right. Then they spent the rest of the time arguing about who was smarter.

"I'm smarter, knucklehead," Dunglap said.

"I don't think so, dimwit," said Mervis.

"Look who's calling who a dimwit, you nitwit!" yelled Dunglap.

Rancid finally ordered Mervis and Dunglap to take their argument outside.

Meanwhile, Cat knew the answers to some difficult history questions, especially the ones about Egypt. But Cat didn't get any points for his correct answers. When Cat wasn't looking, Cliff broke Cat's buzzer. Then Cliff would just repeat Cat's answers after Cat shouted them out.

"You must use your buzzer," Mr. Sunshine reminded Cat.

"But it's broken!" Cat cried.

"Those are the rules," Rancid instructed.

"Arrggghhh!!!!" exclaimed Cat.

CatDog didn't know what they were up against. They didn't know what other dirty tricks the Greasers had up their dirty sleeves.

The next questions were math problems. Each team was given paper and pencils.

"All right, Dog, we can still win this contest," Cat whispered. "Let me use your buzzer instead."

But changing buzzers wouldn't help. One question after another was answered correctly by the Greasers!

"What's going on?" Cat wondered. "They're Greasers, after all—not Einstein!"

Suddenly CatDog heard a very faint "Heh, heh" coming from behind them.

Cat spun around to see Winslow sitting there. "Where have you been? You're supposed to be on our team!" Then Cat noticed that Winslow was holding a huge mirror—just the perfect size to reflect every answer they wrote on paper back to the Greasers!

"Why, you little rat!" began Cat, narrowing his eyes. "How could you go behind our back like that?"

"Hey, the Greasers pay well," said Winslow. "A guy's gotta make a living! Later, losers!"

Cat could no longer concentrate. Worse, the Greasers won the last round of questions. Out of nowhere, Lube was answering all of the Spanish questions in perfect Spanish!

"Who knew!?" Cat said in disbelief.

"And the winning team is the Greasers!" announced Randolph. "In fact, they win all fifty contests in the smarts competition!"

"Hooray!" yelled the crowd.

"Ugh," said CatDog.

Chapter Seven

"Next up, sports fans, are the games competitions," Randolph announced. "We'll begin with the boxing contest."

Then Randolph's voice changed and he sounded like an announcer at a real boxing match, "And in this corner . . . is the undisputed heavyweight champion and all-around bully . . . Cliff!"

"Boo!" the audience hissed.

Cliff growled at the audience and the booing quickly turned into cheering for him.

Randolph continued, "And in this corner . . . a lightweight competing in his debut fight . . . Cat!"

"Hooray!" cheered Dog. He was the only one, though.

Mr. Sunshine hit a small bell and the fight began.

Two seconds later, Randolph was back on the microphone. "The world records have been won by Cliff for quickest knockout—and shortest fight!"

"Way to go, boss!" cheered Shriek.

"Thanks," replied Cliff, looking around.

If the Greasers were going to keep winning, Cliff knew he had to get rid of the competition. He saw Eddie the Squirrel putting on a pair of boxing gloves. "Hey, Eddie!" he called.

"Great fight, Cliff," said Eddie. "I've been working on my moves for when I become a Greaser."

"Yous can't be a Greaser by competin'

against me!" Cliff told him.

Eddie had to think fast. "Well, can I *join* your team?" he asked.

"Yeah . . . sure . . . as my punching bag!" Cliff laughed as he lunged toward Eddie.

Eddie hightailed it out of there—for good!

Meanwhile, Dog was taking care of Cat. "You okay, Cat?" Dog asked his brother.

"Yeah, sure," replied Cat, still seeing stars. He took a deep breath. "I let 'em win."

Dog looked confused.

"It will make our success so much sweeter," Cat whispered. "It's all about a comeback."

Dog shrugged. "Oh."

Then all of a sudden, they heard Winslow say, "Thanks, CatDog."

CatDog turned to see Winslow

counting a wad of money.

"Good thing I bet against you, Cat," Winslow explained. "You've made me very rich!"

"You'll be sorry you went to the enemy when we win!" Cat threatened.

"Yeah, sure!" Winslow replied. "I'll believe it when I see it!"

Dog pulled Cat aside. "We're not doing so good, Cat," he said.

Cat wasn't about to give up. "We'll win this thing if it's the last thing I do!" he declared.

But CatDog didn't have much luck in the rest of the games category. They had no chance in the surfing competition because Cat hated water. And it turned out that Shriek was a classically trained synchronized swimmer and won that contest hands down!

In the checkers contest, it was Cat versus Lube.

"Uh, what color am I?" asked Lube.

"Red," answered Cat. "You go first."

"Uh, what color am I?" asked Lube.

"Red," Cat repeated.

"Oh . . . right," said Lube.

Ten minutes later, Lube still hadn't made a move. Cat couldn't stand it any longer. "Go!" he shouted. "It's your turn!"

"Uh, what color am I?" asked Lube.

"Red! Red! RED!" screamed Cat.

"Oh . . . heh, heh . . . like your face," Lube replied with a chuckle. And he finally moved a red piece and the game began.

A few minutes later, Cat was actually winning! He was just about to make history by completing the most checker jumps in one turn. But disaster struck . . .

The other teams were warming up for

the fetch competition. The Greasers made sure that Dog saw the rubber balls being tossed around. And their sneaky plan worked!

"Whoa!" yelled Cat as Dog chased after a ball.

As Dog dragged Cat away from the checker game, the checkerboard and all the pieces went flying.

"And the winner by default is Lube!" Randolph announced.

"Dooooog!" screamed Cat.

"Oops. Sorry," said Dog. "I couldn't help myself."

At the same time, another noisy racket was going on nearby. Mervis and Dunglap were in a loud argument over the rules of miniature golf. Finally, Rancid couldn't stand them anymore. He gave Mervis and Dunglap honorary awards for most annoying arguments—and then promptly disqualified them from the rest of the competitions.

The final contest in the games category was a baseball game. Whoever hit the most home runs on a team would win the contest.

The problem was that there weren't enough contestants to make up two teams. It was down to the Greasers and CatDog.

Cliff thought it was a perfect time for his favorite song. "Beat Cat up at the ball game, beat Cat up in the crowd," he sang. All the Greasers joined in. Then the audience even joined in!

"Turr-rrific," Cat said, annoyed. "You know, we've gotta get a new theme song."

"Play ball!" Randolph announced.

But CatDog never had a chance. The Greasers played rough, including stealing all

the bases so CatDog could never complete a home run. The Greasers actually picked up the bases and hid them!

The Greasers were on a winning streak!

Chapter Eight

The next day, things weren't going any better. Every time Cat was close to winning a contest, something seemed to go wrong.

In the bizarre-and-unusual category, the Greasers won the juggling chainsaws contest, the longest-you-can-lean-back-on-the-legs-of-a-chair contest, and in a very close race, Lube beat out Dog in the throwing-cereal-up-in-the-air-and-catching-it-in-your-mouth contest.

"Good thing you're tall," Shriek said to Lube.

"Yeah," agreed Lube. "And, uh, hungry!"

Cat was getting desperate. "Just one!

Let us win one contest!" he cried to himself.

The Greasers made their way over to CatDog.

"Hey, why not save yourselves from more embarrassment and just give up?" Shriek suggested, gloating.

"Yeah," agreed Cliff. "You got no chance now. We're winnin' by a landslide."

But Cat stood firm. "CatDog *never* gives up," he said proudly. "You don't know what you're up against."

The Greasers started to laugh.

"We're up against nothin'!" said Cliff. "The score is 156 to 0!"

"Dis here is da easiest contest we ever won!" Shriek gloated.

"And duh Greasers *always* win!" added Lube.

Still laughing, the Greasers left to prepare for the next set of competitions.

Cat was upset. "Maybe the Greasers are right," he said with a sigh. "We're never going to win a competition."

Dog hadn't heard his brother talk like this before. "Cat, we can't give up now," he said. "A wise guy once said, 'Losers never win.'"

Cat did a double take. "Wait a minute. *I* said that."

"That's right," said Dog. "You did."

Cat thought for a moment and then grinned at Dog. With a deep breath and renewed energy, he said, "Let's go! We're going to make a world-record comeback!"

Chapter Nine

The next category was the dance competition.

"Okay, Dog," said Cat, "I think we can really make a comeback in this category. There are 157 dance competitions. If we win all of them, then we'll beat the Greasers."

"Well, we've got four feet," said Dog. "All the easier to dance with!"

"And *win* with!" added Cat. "I'll do one dance and then you dance the next. That way we'll never get tired," said Cat as they high-fived.

Mayor Rancid, Randolph Grant, the TV crews, and the public had all filed into an indoor ballroom.

"Hello again," one reporter said to a

TV camera. "This is Barbara Dingleberry live from the Nearburg Ballroom. We're continuing our special team coverage of this incredible day in Nearburg history. Harry, how does it look from where you are?"

Harry Wisenhymer was standing only five feet from Barbara Dingleberry. "Well, it looks pretty much the same over here," said Harry. "Let's check in with our special correspondent Sheldon Halfwit."

"Thank you, Harry," replied Sheldon. "I'm standing just across from you on the south side of the ballroom. And I'm happy to say that things look *exactly* the same over here. Back to you, Barbara."

"Thank you for those in-depth reports," said Barbara. "Oh! The dancers are just about to begin. But we'll keep our team coverage going and bring our viewers all the breaking news."

Finally, Randolph took the microphone. "Hey there you cool cats, it's time for the big dance competition! Every song will be a different style of dancing, which I will announce. At the end of each song, I will announce a winner."

Mayor Rancid grabbed the microphone. "So get out there and boogie!"

Mr. Sunshine, who was in charge of the music, put on the first song. It was a two-step.

"So amateur," said Cat rolling his eyes. "Dog could do this in his sleep."

And Cat was right. They won the two-step contest! After suffering one defeat after another, CatDog had finally won a contest!

"We won! We won!" cheered Dog.

"I knew we had it in us!" cried Cat.

"I'm sure it was just a fluke," Shriek said.

"Well, we'll see about that," answered Cat as the jitterbug dance began.

CatDog won that one, too!

"Good job!" Dog told Cat.

"I do what I can," replied Cat with a smirk.

Surprisingly, CatDog began to win quite a few of the dances! They mastered the tango and the foxtrot. They wowed everyone with their salsa dancing, tap dancing, and hula dancing.

On the other hand, the Greasers seemed to be better at bullying than they were at dancing. Lube went down in the rumba, Shriek took a fall in the samba, and Cliff just plain refused to ballroom dance.

There were also unusual dances that CatDog won. They easily won the longest-time-dancing dance, the napping-while-you-dance dance, and Dog's favorite, the eating-while-you-dance dance.

"Hey! Save your appetite," Cat warned Dog. "The eating contest is later."

"Don't worry," said Dog. "You know me—I'm always hungry!"

Much to everyone's surprise, the CatDog comeback had worked! The score was tied 156 to 156. There was only one more dance.

The Greasers were looking pretty harried. Lube had a cast on his leg and Shriek had a cast on her face. It was all up to Cliff.

"Come on, boss," Shriek said to Cliff. "You can't let dat CatDog win. We're so close. You gotta get out dere and dance."

Lube agreed. "Besides, dancin' is fun."

Cliff pointed to Lube's cast and said, "Yeah, sure it is." But Cliff knew the Greasers' reputation was at stake. He couldn't be beaten by CatDog—even if that meant having to dance!

The final dance contest was disco. CatDog hurriedly changed into white suits, and black shirts with wide collars.

"Looks are everything," Cat told Dog. "This 70s outfit will definitely impress the judges!"

"Watch out John Travolta!" shouted Dog.

Cat got excited, too. "This CatDog's got *Saturday Night Fever*!"

Dog paused. "But it's Sunday," he said, confused.

"Oh, come on!" Cat said in exasperation. "We've got a disco contest to win!"

With that, the colored lights came on, the mirror ball dropped down, and the disco dancing began.

CatDog took to the floor and showed

off their best moves. Cliff, on the other hand, had no rhythm. He never had any rhythm, and it seemed he never would. He was immediately disqualified.

Randolph spoke into the microphone. "It looks like this last dance is going to be a breeze for CatDog, who seems to have all the right moves."

Cat couldn't be happier. "See, Dog, I told you we'd score big eventually. And at the end of this song, we'll finally be ahead of those lousy Greasers."

"You are always right, Cat," Dog told him.

"That's what I keep telling you!" Cat replied. Then he thought aloud, "Well, since this dance is such a cinch why get all sweaty? I hate being sweaty." He began to dance a little slower and less energetically.

Suddenly Randolph said, "Wait!

What's this? Who is this new super disco dancer?"

Everyone turned to see a funny-looking man. He couldn't keep his feet from dancing to the beat. It was Mr. Sunshine! The audience began clapping and cheering for Mr. Sunshine. The spotlight came on and a disco star was born!

"Well, disco fans, I think we know who our winner is!" Randolph exclaimed. "The new king of disco—Mr. Sunshine!"

Cat couldn't believe his ears! "Nooooooo!" he cried. He was so humiliated.

Everyone crowded around Mr. Sunshine.

"That's my right-hand man!" Rancid declared to the crowd.

"But he wasn't even entered in the contest!" Cat complained.

"*I* make the rules," Rancid reminded him. Then he whispered to Mr. Sunshine, "I never knew this side of you. Let's talk later on how to use it in my re-election campaign."

No one cared that CatDog had won 156 out of 157 dances. The overall score was now tied between the Greasers and CatDog: 156 to 156. And there was only one more competition to go. . . .

Chapter Ten

"I'm sure we'll win this contest, Cat," Dog said. "It's food, after all!"

Cat was moping. He hadn't fully recovered from the shock of losing the disco dance contest.

Dog thought quickly. "And it's tacos! My favorite!"

"Hmmm," Cat began. "You have a point there, my canine friend."

The last competition was a how- many- tacos- can- you -in- one- sitting contest. By this time, all of the other contestants had dropped out or had been disqualified. It was a showdown between CatDog and the Greasers. Dog would represent CatDog, and Lube would represent the Greasers. With the score tied, whoever won this last contest would be crowned Most World Records Holder.

Cat sprang into action. "All right, this is it. This is what we've worked for. Do you feel ready?"

Dog grinned. "Ready—and hungry!"

Just then Randolph announced the beginning of the taco-eating contest. "The only rule is to eat, eat, and then when you're finished, eat some more!"

"Hi-ho-diggety!" cheered Dog.

"Eat your way into the record books!" Cat told Dog.

A bell rang and the chowing began!

Randolph kept score as if he was watching a horse race. "And they're off. Dog's in front with thirty tacos. But Lube is coming up from behind. Dog is vacuuming those tacos up. Lube's mouth has stretched to new limits as he shovels more and more tacos into his mouth. Dog is in the lead with 217. Lube is right behind him with 201. . . ."

"Come on, Dog!" cheered Cat. "You can do it!"

Unfortunately for Lube, the cheering messed up his concentration. "Duh . . . where was I . . . 201 . . . no, uh, was it 102?"

Meanwhile, Dog kept eating and eating. He was up to 800 tacos!

Suddenly Cat felt something—and it didn't feel good. "Uh-oh," he said quietly. "Uh, Dog? You might want to slow down a little."

But there was no stopping Dog. All he saw were plates and plates full of tacos . . . 821 . . . 822 . . . 823. It's as if his eyes were bigger than his stomach.

And then his stomach was bigger than anything!

Before anyone knew what was

happening, Cat's mouth opened and all 823 tacos came flying out! They landed all over Mayor Rancid, Randolph, and the entire audience.

"Oops," said Dog.

"Oops is right," piped up Winslow. "That is one taco grande meal! Heh! Heh!"

"I guess this means we didn't win?" Dog asked hesitantly.

Cat nodded. "This means we start running—NOW!"

When the Nearburg Book of World Records finally came out, CatDog *did* get mentioned. But it wasn't what they had hoped for.

Under the picture of the infamous taco incident, the caption read, "Those who provided the grossest day in Nearburg history!"